The Two-Horse Cadillac

Zig Ziglar with Annie Regan

Tyndale House Publishers, Inc.   Wheaton, Illinois

Illustrations by Mary Beth Schwark
First printing, September 1987
Library of Congress Catalog Card Number 87-50829
ISBN 0-8423-7388-8
Copyright 1987 by Zig Ziglar
Printed in the United States of America

The Contest

Hometown Pride Contest, the banner said. Windy McGraw skidded to a halt and perched on her bicycle to watch a man in overalls struggle with it. An August breeze against him, he finally stretched it from the mayor's office to the drugstore, forming a canopy across Main Street.

"Tell us about your hometown," Windy read on, "and be featured on television."

That's all? she wondered, pedaling forward. *I just tell them about Three Forks and they'll put me on television?* The town's history came to mind, the hustle and bustle when it had been a busy river port. *Of course, it's different now,* Windy thought. *The river changed course and left Three Forks a small town where not much happens.*

She parked her bike in front of the mayor's

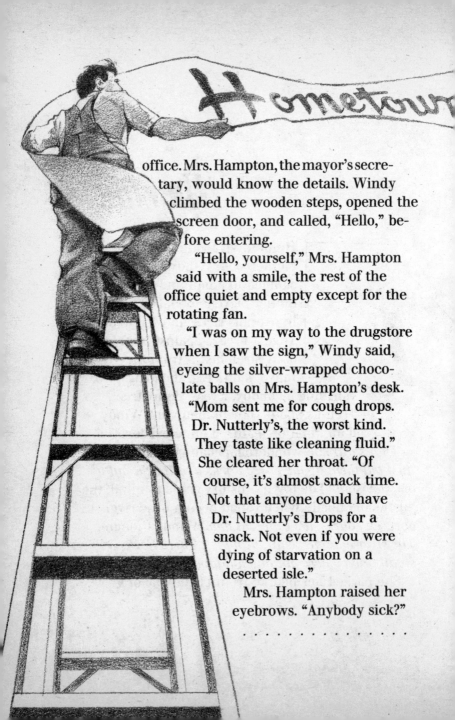

office. Mrs. Hampton, the mayor's secretary, would know the details. Windy climbed the wooden steps, opened the screen door, and called, "Hello," before entering.

"Hello, yourself," Mrs. Hampton said with a smile, the rest of the office quiet and empty except for the rotating fan.

"I was on my way to the drugstore when I saw the sign," Windy said, eyeing the silver-wrapped chocolate balls on Mrs. Hampton's desk. "Mom sent me for cough drops. Dr. Nutterly's, the worst kind. They taste like cleaning fluid." She cleared her throat. "Of course, it's almost snack time. Not that anyone could have Dr. Nutterly's Drops for a snack. Not even if you were dying of starvation on a deserted isle."

Mrs. Hampton raised her eyebrows. "Anybody sick?"

. . . .

she asked, returning to her paperwork.

"Pete feels like he might have a sore throat. My mom likes to be prepared." Windy sat down in an orange plastic chair. "Shorty Holden says if you don't have cough drops, you can just eat dry graham crackers or shredded wheat."

Mrs. Hampton looked up.

"He says it'll scratch the itch on the way down," Windy explained. Now that she had Mrs. Hampton's attention, she gazed at the chocolate balls again. "Of course, candy would be better. Any kind would give you something to suck on."

"That's interesting." Mrs. Hampton reached for the jar of chocolates. "Of course, it's Peter who has the sore throat." She took an envelope from her desk, filled it with candy, and sealed it shut. "Tell him it's from me," she said with a grin. "Maybe he'll share."

"Thanks," Windy laughed, accepting the envelope. *Why do I have to be so obvious?* she thought as she stood to leave. Then remembering why she'd come, she asked, "I was wondering about the contest. How does it work?"

"The governor has declared October to be Hometown Pride Month," Mrs. Hampton said.

"Each town is to come up with an entry demonstrating what's special about it. The entries will compete at the county level. The winners will go up against each other in the state capitol. The town that finally wins gets a plaque naming it Hometown of the Year. The governor will visit for a day of festivities, which will be featured in a television special."

Mrs. Hampton finished in a matter-of-fact tone. "Of course, Three Forks won't win. But it's the mayor's job to let everyone know what's going on. You can help by telling your friends. Pass the word around."

"Thanks. I will." Windy waved good-bye. "I'm off to the drugstore and then back home to give Pete his choice. See you later." She stepped outside and closed the screen door slowly to keep it from banging.

Pete was waiting on the front porch when Windy arrived. "What took you so long?" he asked, a whine to his voice. "I could be dying."

"I stopped to see Mrs. Hampton. She sent you these." Windy tore the top off the envelope and held it for Pete to look inside. "I've got cough drops, too, but they're Dr. Nutterly's. Which would you rather have?"

"Is that a real question?" Pete grabbed the envelope, shook out two chocolate balls, unwrapped one and popped it into his mouth.

"You aren't sick, are you?" Windy asked as she reached for the other chocolate in Pete's hand.

Pete licked his lips. "I'm not sick," he said, emptying the envelope into his shirt pocket.

"Then let's go to Drew and Rachel's." Windy opened the front door. "I'll tell Mom."

Mrs. McGraw was in the basement, sorting through donations to the church's parking lot sale. "Have fun," she said when Windy told her where they were going. "I thought Pete might feel better when you came back with Dr. Nutterly's Drops."

"Actually, I think it was the chocolate balls Mrs. Hampton sent him." Windy picked up a red taffeta dress and tried it on over her T-shirt and jeans. "I stopped by to ask about the Hometown Pride Contest."

"I heard about it yesterday." Mrs. McGraw frowned at Windy's outfit. "That doesn't fit, honey." She helped her out of the dress. "Anyway, I forgot to mention the contest. It's an interesting idea, but we'll never win. Three Forks is about as ordinary as a small town gets. I'm afraid a town needs to be outstanding to win the contest."

Windy nodded. "I promised Mrs. Hampton I'd help get the word around. I'll tell the Womacks, Sellers, and Holdens. Then I'll forget about it."

"What about Uncle Zig?" Pete tramped into the basement, hearing the last of their conversation on his way down the stairs.

"OK, him too." Windy gave her mother a hug. "But that's all. I'm not the phone company, you know."

Three Forks was a small enough town that it seemed right to pass information along to your neighbors and leave the rest to the natural flow of news. *After all, Three Forks isn't going to win,* Windy thought. *There's no point getting all excited about being on television.*

Shane and Paul Sellers were playing ball with Drew and Rachel in the Womacks' front yard when Pete and Windy rode up. Windy repeated what Mrs. Hampton had told her about the contest and concluded with the obvious. "Of course, Three Forks won't win."

"I'll bet the same people that put on the show for the Fourth of July will enter," Drew said. He sent a gray rock skipping down the driveway. "Like Mrs. Truffles and her talking dog."

"She'll get him to howl along with 'The Star-Spangled Banner,'" Shane said. "Or she'll write a new song about hometowns for the occasion."

"The Hempell twins will throw their batons," Paul added, "and probably break another street-light."

"Nope." Rachel shook her head. "They've been practicing. I saw them yesterday. They're actually getting halfway decent."

"Mr. Carver will grow his mustache to his chin,

wax it until it sticks out like handlebars, and then
recite early American poetry. He's kind of good."
Windy looked doubtful as she said it. The children
knew all the people in town longed to be in show
business. Although they were enthusiastic, they
just weren't very good.

"We need someone who can compete with professionals," Shane said. "Some towns have people
who are actually in show business."

"Mr. and Mrs. Hartsog will square dance," Paul
said, continuing the list.

"Too bad he'll step on her toes."

"The Seifords will play 'America the Beautiful' on
their horns."

"Miss Charmain
will model turn-
of-the-century
fashions."

"Let's face it,"
Rachel con-
cluded. "We like
ourselves in
this town be-
cause we know
ourselves, but
people who don't
know us . . ."
She grinned
and shrugged.

. . . .

"I heard the mayor say the other day that he thinks we have spunk." Windy held the tip of her nose. "The judges might think it's skunk." She laughed and blessed Drew with a handful of grass over his head. "We've got skunk, we've got skunk," she singsonged as he chased her down the drive.

"She's right," Rachel said. "Three Forks will never win the contest. Let's just forget it."

The Old Man's Cadillac

The following week proved the children right. Mrs. Hampton posted a sign-up sheet in the mayor's office. "TRYOUTS," it said in bold letters. "Help present our town in the Hometown Pride Contest." All the usual people signed up.

The mayor looked at the list every day and laughed. "I guess that's what America is all about," he'd say. "Everybody gets a shot at the big time."

By Saturday, the children had almost forgotten the contest. Rachel answered the phone early in the morning to find Uncle Zig on the other end. "I'm home," his deep voice boomed, "and my swimming pool's empty. Think you can do something about it?"

"I'll work on it." Rachel replied with a grin. By

ten o'clock, Uncle Zig's pool was filled with nine children diving and splashing in the cool water. Uncle Zig sat sunning himself by the pool and talking on the telephone until Aunt Jean appeared with eleven glasses of pink lemonade.

"This day's full of problems," he called over the children's shouts and laughter. "First, an empty pool. And now, eleven glasses of lemonade with only two of us to drink them."

"We'll work on it," Rachel and Windy yelled as they chased each other out of the pool.

"Windy, weren't you supposed to tell Uncle Zig something?" Pete said, scrambling after them. "A couple days ago when you said you weren't the telephone company."

Windy thought for a second, then remembered the contest. "It's the Hometown Pride Contest," she said as she grabbed her lemonade. She explained about the contest beween sips. "Anyway, Three Forks won't win even the county competition," she concluded. "No way!"

"Now you did it," Drew growled under his breath. "Never say, 'No way!' to him."

The children turned toward Uncle Zig, the determined look on his face telling them Drew was

right. "No way never got anywhere" was one of his favorite sayings. He believed it with his whole heart.

"But this time it's true," Shane said. "Tell him who's on the tryout sheet, Windy."

"Well, there's Mr. and Mrs. Hartsog," Windy began, calling off the entries as they came to mind. When she finished, Uncle Zig was frowning but still looking determined.

"We need somebody who can compete with professionals," Shane said.

"The mayor keeps looking at the list and saying, 'That's what America is all about. Everybody gets a shot at the big time,'" Rachel added. "But then he laughs because he knows . . ."

". . . This town doesn't have any talent," Pete finished.

"And there's nothing special

about it," Windy said with feeling, remembering the way it used to be. "Not anymore. Three Forks used to be a river town. It forked off in three directions right there. But now it's gone, and we're just about as ordinary as a hometown can be."

Uncle Zig ran his hands through his hair, clicked off the ringer on his telephone, stretched back in his lawn chair, and took a long sip of lemonade. Then he cleared his throat and said quietly, "I don't suppose you've heard about the two-horse Cadillac."

Drew grinned as they settled around the pool for a story. It would be entertaining. Uncle Zig's tales always were. *But this time it won't change anything,* he thought. *Nothing can make Three Forks different from what it is.*

"Some time ago, an old man in Oklahoma discovered oil on his land," Uncle Zig began. "All his life he'd been penniless, but the oil suddenly made him a very wealthy man. The first thing he did with his new money was to buy a big Cadillac touring car.

"In those days, touring car convertibles had two spare tires on the back. However, the old man wanted the longest car in Oklahoma, so he added four more spare tires.

"Then he bought an Abraham Lincoln stovepipe hat, a coat with long tails, and a bow tie. He completed his outfit with a big black cigar." Uncle Zig paused to finish his drink.

"Every day the old man would drive into the hot, dusty little cowtown nearby." Uncle Zig crossed his legs at the ankles and continued. "He wanted to see everyone and wanted everyone to see him. He was a friendly old soul. As he rode through town, he would stand up in the car and turn in both directions, left and right, to speak to everyone in sight. In fact, he would turn all the way around if someone was behind him. Still, he never ran into anyone or anything."

Uncle Zig stopped to let the children guess the reason why.

"He was a very good driver?" Paul asked.

Uncle Zig shook his head. "He never even learned how to steer."

"He had a chauffeur," Windy suggested.

"Nope. He rode all by himself."

"He ran out of gas when he got to town. Then he just parked the car on Main Street and talked to people." Drew laughed at his own answer. It was all he could think of.

"Actually, he never bought gas for the car," Uncle Zig said. "Remember what I told you in the beginning? I said it was a two-horse Cadillac."

"He had two horses pull his car?" Windy asked in astonishment. "Why would he do that?"

"Exactly!" Uncle Zig beamed. "The old man never learned how to turn the key and switch on the ignition. Local mechanics said there was noth-

ing wrong with the car's engine. Inside there was a hundred horsepower engine ready, willing, and raring to go.

"The old man had invested a fortune in his Cadillac. He'd paid for the best car in the land. But instead of using the horsepower inside the engine, he'd used the horsepower on the outside—two ancient, broken-down nags almost as old as he was."

Uncle Zig stood up, reached for his glasses on the table next to the lawn chair, and looked at his wife. "Mind if I go inside, dear?" he asked, ignoring the children's bewildered expressions. "Let the kids have another romp in the pool before they go home."

"The point!" Drew couldn't help yelling. "What's the point? You can't leave us without explaining what the two-horse Cadillac has to do with Three Forks and the Hometown Pride Contest."

"It's simple," Uncle Zig said with amusement.

"Lots of people make the mistake of looking outside themselves to find two horsepower when they should look inside where they have over a hundred. Experts tell us we use only about 5 percent of the ability we have.

"You've been looking at Three Forks from the outside, looking for talent to compete with 'professionals' and not finding it. You've been shaking your heads at the odd assortment of people on the tryout list. But the mayor's right. Three Forks is what America is all about. If you stop looking at our town on the outside, you'll discover the true talent that lies at its heart."

He stopped for a moment, contemplating the children one by one. "The same thing is true for each of you," he said in a thoughtful voice. "None of you can sing, dance, or play a musical instrument, and so you conclude that nobody has talent.

"But, Drew, I haven't met a better organizer. Think about the school paper drive, the car wash,

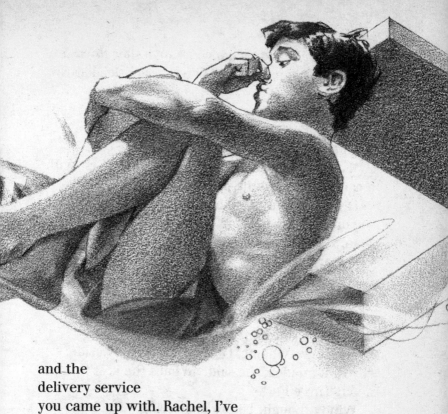

and the
delivery service
you came up with. Rachel, I've
got your drawings in my study. And Windy, you
can always think of a poem. Pete, . . ." One by
one, he called out their names, mentioning something special about each.

"I'm not saying Three Forks will win the contest,"
he added as he walked toward his back door, "but
if we all do our best with what we have, we'll be
winners anyway. You know *that's* what winners
are . . . people who do their best! Besides, Three

Forks has as good a chance as any other town in America. If you ask me, Three Forks is loaded with talent!"

"I have a half hour to spare." Aunt Jean turned to the children. "Back in the water unless you want to waste it."

"Follow the leader," Pete called, going first with a cannonball into the pool.

Drew took his place behind Rachel in line for the diving board. While he waited, he asked Aunt Jean, "Why does he always do that? Make us think backward?"

She laughed. "That's what he does," she said. "He makes people think what they *can* do instead of what they *think* they can't do. He likes to say, 'You *can* if you *think* you can.' "

On the way home, Drew called Windy aside. "I've got an idea," he said. "What's the best thing about Three Forks?"

Windy thought before answering. "The best thing about Three Forks is that people care about each other," she said slowly. "And they watch out for each other. Like the time Cissy Lewis got lost. Everybody stopped to look for her, even the mayor."

"That's exactly what I've been thinking," Drew said. "If we could get people to understand that . . ." Excitement rippled through his voice. "If we could somehow show that, it would be the best of all. Isn't that what hometowns are for?"

"Hey, guys!" Windy called to the others, motioning for them to slow down. "What do you think of this idea?" By the time the children had gone home for lunch, they were already working on a plan.

The Plan

CHAPTER

3

"We're nuts," Pete told Windy at home. "How can kids convince people that love is what's special about Three Forks? And even if we do, how will it work?"

He took a bite of his sandwich and continued. "What are we going to do? We could stand up in a row at the county contest and say, 'We're from Three Forks, but that's OK because we really care about each other—and you'd better believe it!'" He lowered his voice and added, "'Or we'll bop you on the head!'"

Windy laughed. "We could line up in the shape of a heart, like the Coke Christmas tree commercial, and sing, 'We want to teach the world to love like people in Three Forks do.'" She hummed the tune.

. . . .

"Or we could invent a love bomb." Pete's imagination spun out. "We could discover some kind of chemical that makes people nice to each other, stick it in little balls that disintegrate on contact, and plaster everybody with them."

The silliness continued until Windy said in a serious tone, "I guess you're right. It's almost impossible to make a presentation out of love."

"What's impossible?" Mrs. McGraw asked from the kitchen.

As Windy explained, her mother came to sit beside them. "Your plan's a good one," Mrs. Mcgraw said when Windy finished. "Don't give it up." She thought for a moment, then look a of inspiration brightened her face. "Miss Spenser might be able to help. She's lived in Three Forks all her life. She was a schoolteacher in the old days, you know, and has some wonderful stories to tell. Maybe she could help you put a play together—"

"Mother," Pete interrupted, "Miss Spenser is pretty old."

"Exactly." Mrs. McGraw stood and began clearing

the dishes. "Don't you remember how you visited her when we lived across town? How she baked cookies for you and told you stories about the old days? She's as sharp and clearheaded as ever. She knows about Three Forks the way it was and the way it is."

Pete and Windy helped their mother with the clearing and then went to sit on the back steps. Neither of them wanted to say what they were thinking, but finally Pete whispered, "We haven't visited Miss Spenser in a long time. If we go now, she'll think we just want something."

Windy nodded. "When we moved, we promised to visit at least once a month. Funny, it seems so far across town now. I guess we've been lazy because we've made lots of friends on this block."

"I wonder how she's doing," Pete said with hesitation.

"I'm doing fine, thanks." Rachel poked her head around the

corner of the house. "But I came to talk to you about our idea. Drew and I aren't sure it can really work."

"Well," Windy said, wondering if she should mention Miss Spenser. "My mom had an idea."

"I'm all ears." Rachel cupped her hands to her ears. "Even the part of me that's not."

When Windy had explained about Miss Spenser, Rachel said, "Let's get Drew and visit her. It can't hurt."

Miss Spenser was swinging on her front porch when the children arrived. Dressed in a frilly skirt with pearls and a wide-brimmed hat, she looked ready to have her picture taken. Twelve cats decorated her gray-and-white porch. Windy counted them and elbowed Pete. "She's adopted four more since we left," she whispered.

"Seven more," Pete whispered back, pointing to three other cats on the shingled roof.

Miss Spenser seemed delighted to see them. "Windy and Pete!" she exclaimed, patting her gloved hands together. "How long has it been?"

Pete and Windy blushed, but Miss Spenser continued. "It doesn't matter," she said. "Any time is too long. You're two of my favorite people. Come in. All of you, please come in. I just baked a fresh batch of oatmeal-raisin cookies."

She beamed at the group. Then a worried look crossed her face. "Of course, I have chocolate-chip cookies and caramel swirls in the cookie jar if you don't like oatmeal-raisin," she said.

When the four children were seated in Miss Spenser's kitchen, sipping cold chocolate milk and munching on cookies, Miss Spenser said, "Now to what do I owe the pleasure of this visit? Or did you stroll across town just to see me?"

"I guess we didn't," Windy admitted with embarrassment. "We have a problem, and my mom thought maybe you could help."

"Then no time for idle chitchat." Miss Spenser folded her hands in a listening position, her elbows on the kitchen table and her chin against her knuckles. "I'm all ears except for the part of me that isn't."

Rachel laughed. "I thought I was the only one who said that," she said, then told their story from the beginning of Windy's visit to the mayor's office. "So you see," she finished, "everyone thought there was no way Three Forks could win the contest. But Uncle Zig got us thinking in a different direction. We came up with a plan for showing how much people in Three Forks care about each other, but now we can't figure how to make it work."

"I see." Miss Spenser leaned on her knuckles and stared out the window, deep in thought. "I see," she said again, the *see* whistling as it passed her lips.

The kitchen was quiet except for the ticktock of the cuckoo clock as the children waited in silence.

Miss Spenser closed her eyes and was quiet so long that Pete almost asked if she was asleep. But Rachel put a finger to her lips, motioning for him to wait a bit longer.

Finally, Miss Spenser opened her eyes. "Three Forks is full of stories, from the beginning until now," she said with a smile. "Let's weave them together and come up with something wonderful. Follow me." She stood, motioning for them to rise. "This way." She turned and walked past the pantry to a small yellow door. "This leads to the attic," she said as she opened the door. "There are attics like this all over town."

Miss Spenser's attic was a low narrow room running the length of her home. As the children climbed the steep stairs, it seemed as if they were traveling back through time. The room was crammed with things from bygone days.

Miss Spenser scooped a small pair of white skates from a shelf near the entrance. "My first pair of skates," she exclaimed. "And my brother's bicycle." She pointed to a funny-looking contraption across the room. "I could sit here and remember for days."

"But I brought you up to show you that it's full of things from the past. And it's not the only attic like this. I've no doubt we can round up enough costumes and props to tell our story from the beginning."

The children poked and snooped through the attic for the next hour, remarking at each new discovery. Miss Spenser, at seventy-five and still a teacher, answered all their questions, explaining the details. Finally, she led them back down to the kitchen.

"Let's make a list," she said when they were seated at the table again. She went to a drawer and pulled out a pen and some paper. "First of all, what's our goal?" She searched their faces. "What do we want to accomplish with this play?"

Drew answered. "We want to show the history of Three Forks. How it began as a busy river town and turned into a quiet family town. How it's made up of people that care. Just ordinary people . . ."

". . . Maybe even kind of funny people like Mrs. Truffles with her singing dog," Rachel added, "but people who care about each other."

"How even though we're not very important to outsiders, we're important to each other," Windy said.

Pete nodded. "And it's the everyday acts of kindness that make us glad we live here."

Miss Spenser scribbled as the children spoke. Then she said, "We'll tell it just like that. You children will be narrators. We'll begin it just the way it happened with Windy visiting the mayor's office, all the amateur showmen signing up, and everyone thinking Three Forks had no chance of winning."

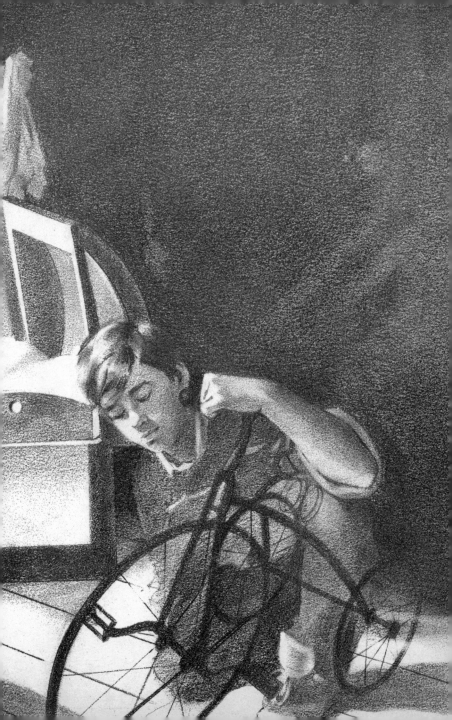

She spoke with growing excitement. "We can even include your talk with Uncle Zig and his story about the two-horse Cadillac. Then we'll roll out our history as seen through the eyes of the people who have lived here. All the stories will be true, some from newspaper clippings and some from word of mouth.

"You can go home now." Miss Spenser put the pen and paper away. "Let the other children know about our talk, then begin working on your opening presentation. Make it easy and natural, just the way it happened. Contact Uncle Zig and ask him if he's willing to tell his story, too."

CAFE

WANTED
THREE FORKS
STORIES/HISTOR

Miss Spenser opened the back door and the children lined up as if they were her students and her kitchen was a classroom. "ll take care of the mayor," she said. "I've known him since he was your age. I'm sure he'll go along with us on this."

In the weeks to come, Miss Spenser and the children spent hours combing Three Forks for stories. Ads, flyers, and posters spread about town brought firsthand accounts of generous deeds. The town library with its collection of old newspapers filled in the rest. As the list grew, they began to marvel at the richness of human kindness that made up the loving atmosphere they'd known all their lives.

Finally the presentation was ready, the script telling of everything from sharing food to saving lives. The actors, some playing themselves, were to bring their characters to life on a simple stage with a minimum of props.

On the afternoon of the final rehearsal, the day before the county competition, Windy found Uncle Zig at the back of the high school auditorium. "I've been thinking about how this whole thing got started," she said. "We were sure Three Forks could never come up with a decent entry, but then you told us about the two-horse Cadillac. That helped us to look at our town from the inside out rather than from the outside in."

She took a deep breath. "I guess what I want to say is that it's changed people around here a little."

She hesitated and went on. "I've been watching how they greet each other now. It's as if they feel prouder, more sure of themselves.

"Maybe it's just my imagination, but I think people hold their heads higher now. Even if we don't win, this Hometown Pride Contest will have been worth the work. It's made us realize how special our town is and given us a chance to appreciate what we usually take for granted."

Uncle Zig looked down at her with pleasure. "That's quite a speech, Windy girl," he said. "And I think it's the perfect ending for the play. We needed a little something at the end, a short postscript. Do you mind if I pass it along to Miss Spenser?"

"Not at all." Windy smiled. "I don't mind who knows what I said."

Before the year was over, the whole state knew what Windy had said. After winning the county competition, Three Forks went on to the state finals where it tied with Hanover City for first place. The television special was filmed in both towns, but when it aired, it closed with Windy's words. "Maybe it's just my imagination, but I think people hold their heads higher now. . . ."

The neighborhood gang watched the special on Uncle Zig's big color television set. "Isn't it great what you can do when you realize you aren't a two-horse Cadillac?" Uncle Zig said when it was through.

The children, lighting up the room with smiles as big as those of jack-o'-lanterns, couldn't have agreed more.

THE END
. . . .